TREASURE
+ ISLAND +

OTHER SCRIBNER STORYBOOK CLASSICS

The Last of the Mohicans
Robinson Crusoe

Atheneum Books for Young Readers

An imprint of Simon & Schuster Children's Publishing Division

1230 Avenue of the Americas

New York, New York 10020

Abridgment copyright © 2003 by Timothy Meis

Illustrations copyright 1911 Simon & Schuster, Inc.

Illustrations copyright renewed 1939

Book design by Abelardo Martínez

The text for this book is set in Palatino.

The illustrations for this book are rendered in oil.

Manufactured in China

First Edition

2 4 6 8 10 9 7 5 3 1

Library of Congress Cataloging-in-Publication Data

Stevenson, Robert Louis.

Treasure island / Robert Louis Stevenson ; illustrated by N. C. Wyeth.—1st ed.

p. cm. — (Scribner storybook classic)

Summary: While going through the possessions of a deceased guest who
owed them money, the mistress of the inn and her son find a treasure map
that leads them to a pirate's fortune.

ISBN 0-689-85468-4

[1. Buried treasure—Fiction. 2. Pirates—Fiction. 3. Adventure and adventurers—Fiction.]

I. Wyeth, N. C. (Newell Convers), 1882–1945 II. Title. III. Series.

PZ7.S8482 Ts 2003

[Fic]—dc21   2002008611

TREASURE
+ ISLAND +

ROBERT LOUIS STEVENSON
illustrated by N. C. WYETH

A SCRIBNER STORYBOOK CLASSIC
Atheneum Books for Young Readers
New York London Toronto Sydney Singapore

A Scale of 3 English Miles

Foremaft Hill

North Inlet

Strong tide here

ye Spye glafs Hill

Skeleton Island

White Rock

Swamp

Spring

Graves

Bulk of treasure here

Cape of ye Woods

Mizzenmaft Hill

Haulbowline Head

Foul Ground

Treasure Island
Augt 1750. J.F.

Given by above J.F. to Mr. W. Bones. Maste of ye Walrus
Savannah this twenty July 1754 W. B.

Facsimile of Chart, latitude and
longitude struck out by J. Hawkins

I had had nightmares about the one-legged man long before I had ever laid eyes upon him. In these visions he was as cruel and heartless as any pirate could be. On stormy nights, when the wind shook the four corners of the house, and the surf roared along the cove and up the cliffs, I would see him in a thousand forms, and with a thousand diabolical expressions. Now the leg would be cut off at the knee, now at the hip; now he was a monstrous kind of creature who had never had but the one leg and that in the middle of his body. The worst of the nightmares was when he would leap and run and pursue me over hill and ditch.

I doubt I would ever have dreamed of, or seen, this scoundrel had it not been for a particular seafaring man who came to my mother's lodging house—the Admiral Benbow Inn. I remember the cold day he arrived as though it were yesterday.

His name was Billy Bones. And with him he brought a rough-and-tumble sea chest, the kind that had seen more corners of the earth than I thought I ever would.

I watched him as he made his way up the road to the Admiral Benbow. He was a tall, strong man whose skin had been colored nut brown by the sun. A pigtail, common for sailors in those days, fell across the broad shoulder of his soiled blue coat.

This is the sea-song that he sang as he walked, and sung so many times afterward.

"Fifteen men on the dead man's chest—
Yo-ho-ho, and a bottle of rum!"

He had a voice that sounded rotted and hollow, as though he had spent a lifetime drinking liquor and shouting down other men. In a moment he was at the door.

He rapped on it with a stick that resembled a capstan from a sailing ship.

I opened the door with more than a little dread and saw across his cheek a white cutlass scar that stood out like a snake on a beach.

"Halloo, matey," he said, placing his wooden trunk at his feet. "Is the man of the inn about?"

"I am he," I replied slowly. For it was true, my father had passed away recently, leaving only my mother and myself to mind the inn.

"What is your name, young fella?"

"Jim Hawkins," I answered.

"I am in need of lodging and rum, Jim Hawkins," he said brusquely. "Have you either?"

"Both."

"Then fetch me some rum, and I shall stay here." He spoke with some authority, as though he were a captain and was used to his orders being obeyed.

I poured a cup of rum and water and brought it to him in the parlor. He held out his closed hand.

"Tell me when I have eaten and drunk through this," he said, and tossed four gold coins upon my tray. I took them up and placed them in my pocket.

"There's another silver fourpenny piece in it for you on the first of each month if you keep an eye out for a one-legged seaman."

I promised that I would and brought his chest to the room he would be occupying.

Over the weeks that he was with us at the inn, I found Billy Bones to be a very silent man by custom. All day he hung round the cove, or upon the cliffs, with a brass telescope; all evening he sat in a corner of the parlor next to the fire, drank rum and water, and blew through his nose like a foghorn. If another seaman stayed at the Admiral Benbow, Bones would peer at him through the curtained door before he entered the parlor.

All day he hung round the cove, or upon the cliffs, with a brass telescope. . . .

I was never scared of Billy Bones, or of the other sailors who came to our inn, but for some reason I was terrified of seeing the one-legged man that Bones told me to watch for. Bones told me little more of him, but he did tell other stories of the sea, dreadful stories about hangings, and walking the plank, and waves that swallowed ships. By his own account he must have lived his life among some of the wickedest men that God ever allowed upon the sea. Occasionally, when drunk, he would ramble on about his sea chest which no one at the inn had ever seen open.

But I was soon to learn what was inside, and that secret would lead me into the greatest adventure I would ever have.

CHAPTER TWO

One day Billy Bones awoke earlier than usual and set out down the beach. His cutlass swung under the broad skirts of the old blue coat; his brass telescope was tucked under his arm; his hat was tilted back upon his head. I remember his breath hanging like smoke in his wake as he strode off.

I was laying the breakfast-table when the parlor door opened, and in stepped a man on whom I had never set my eyes before. He was a pale, tallowy creature, wanting two fingers of the left hand. He was not sailorly, and yet he had a smack of the sea about him. He asked for rum; and as I was going out of the room to fetch it, he sat down at a table.

"Is this here table for the captain?" he asked. "He has a cut on one cheek."

I told him he was out walking.

"Which way, sonny? Which way is he gone?" I pointed toward the beach.

Instead of going after him, though, the stranger just hung about inside the inn door, peering round the corner like a cat waiting for a mouse. He cleared the hilt of his cutlass and loosened the blade in the sheath.

At last in strode Billy Bones, slamming the door behind him. Without looking to the right or left, he marched straight across the room to where his breakfast awaited him.

"Captain," said the stranger, in a voice that I thought he had tried to make bold and big.

Billy Bones spun around and the color drained from his face. Even his nose was blue, for he had the look of a man who sees a ghost. He made a sort of gasp.

"Black Dog!" he said. Then he turned to me, "Get out of here, boy, and don't be spying at the keyhole." I left them, and for a long time I could hear nothing but a low gabble.

Then all of a sudden there was a tremendous explosion of oaths and other noises—the chair and table went over in a lump, a clash of steel followed, and then a cry of pain. In the next instant I saw Black Dog in full flight out the door, blood streaming from his left shoulder, and the captain in hot pursuit with drawn cutlass. Just at the door the captain struck out at the fugitive with one tremendous blow, which would certainly have split him to the chin had not the Admiral Benbow sign gotten in the way.

Black Dog disappeared over the edge of the hill.

"Jim," Billy Bones said, holding himself against the wall, "rum."

"Are you hurt?" I cried.

"Rum," he repeated more loudly. "I must get away from here! Get me rum!"

I ran to fetch it when I heard a loud fall in the parlor, and running in, beheld the captain lying full length upon the floor. My mother, alarmed by the cries, came quickly downstairs to help me. We raised Bones's head. His breathing was short and shallow.

I dashed down the street to fetch Dr. Livesey. When we returned and he examined Bones, the doctor said, "This man has had a stroke."

Between us, with much trouble, we managed to hoist him upstairs and laid him on his bed, where his head fell back on the pillow as if he were almost fainting.

Nearly a day passed before he was capable of moving again. He rose from bed with great difficulty, holding on to my shoulder with a grip that almost made me cry out. But before I could do much to help him, he had fallen back again to his former place, where he lay silent for a while.

"Listen, Jim," he finally said with labored breath. "That Black Dog is a bad one. If I can't get away, and they tip me the black spot, you remember that it's my sea chest they're after."

I didn't understand a word of what he was saying, but he continued.

"I was first mate, I was, old Captain Flint's first mate on the *Walrus*, and I am the only one who knows of the place of the treasure. He gave it to me at Savannah, when he lay a-dying. If Black Dog comes back, it will be the chest he is looking for."

"But what is a black spot, captain?" I asked.

"That's a summons, mate," is all he said. I meant to ask him about the treasure and the chest, but his voice was growing weaker. At length he fell into a heavy, swoonlike sleep. At that point, I left him.

The next morning I was standing at the door when I saw a blind man tapping with a stick, wearing a great green shade over his eyes. He was hunched, as if with age or weakness, and wore a huge old tattered sea-cloak. I never saw in my life a more dreadful-looking figure. He stopped a little from the inn and addressed the air in front of him.

"Will any kind friend inform a poor blind man where he may now be?"

"You are at the Admiral Benbow," said I.

"I hear a young voice," he said. "Will you give me your hand and lead me in?"

I held out my hand, and the horrible creature gripped it like a vise.

"Now, boy," he said, the voice suddenly cruel and cold, "take me to the captain. Lead me straight up to him."

I was so utterly terrified of the blind beggar that I brought him to the sick man's bed. Billy Bones raised his eyes. He made a movement to rise, but I do not believe he had enough force left in his body.

"Now, Bill, stay where you are," said the blind man. "If I can't see, I can hear a finger stirring. Hold out your left hand slowly. Boy, take his left hand by the wrist, and bring it near to my right."

We both obeyed him, and I saw the blind man pass something from the hollow of his hand into the palm of the captain's, which closed upon it instantly.

"And now that's done," said the blind man; and with those words he let go of me, and with incredible accuracy, he left the inn and walked into the road. I could hear his stick go tap-tap-tapping into the distance.

The captain gathered his senses and looked sharply into the palm of his hand at what the blind man put there.

"Eight o'clock!" he cried. "Two hours. They are coming for me!" He sprang to his feet. He reeled, put his hand to his chest, and then fell from his whole height, face forward to the floor. I ran to him at once to help him, but it was in vain. He made not another sound or movement.

Chapter Three

When my mother returned from town shortly after sundown, I told her about all that had transpired with Bones and the blind man, and she rightfully feared for our safety. We could neither go out on the road, nor stay in the house for fear that the murderous pirates would come for Billy Bones and his sea chest and find us. We immediately doused all the lights in the house.

"Pistols," she cried out. "We have none!"

"Perhaps there are some in the seaman's chest," I said, and we both rushed to Bones's room. I went down on my knees at once. On the floor close to the captain's hand was a little round piece of paper, blackened on one side. Taking it up, I found written on the other side, in a very good, clear hand (which told me that the blind man had friends), this short message: YOU HAVE TILL EIGHT TONIGHT.

I instantly became aware of the ticking of the grandfather clock that stood in the parlor. "We haven't much time, mother."

"Jim," she said, almost whispering, "we need a key for the chest."

I felt Bones's pockets, but found nothing.

"Perhaps it's around his neck," suggested my mother.

Overcoming a strong repugnance, I tore open his shirt at the neck, and there, sure enough, hanging to a bit of string, we found the key. My mother took it and quickly opened Billy Bones's chest.

Amid the strong smell of tobacco that wafted from the chest, we found a quadrant, a piece of silver, a pair of compasses, and some other trinkets of little value. But no pistols. Lying on the bottom was a thick piece of paper folded numerous ways. Though I had given no weight to Bones's story of a treasure, I thought this scrap might be some explanation as to why that blind man walked so far just to deliver his black spot.

The clock in the parlor struck.

"Eight o'clock!" I gasped as I stuffed the piece of paper into my shirt. "They'll be here soon."

My mother and I were attempting to return the various items to the seaman's chest when a dreadful sound came from down the road and clutched at my heart. It was the tap-tap-tap of the blind man's cane on the frozen dirt. It drew nearer and nearer while we sat holding our breath. Then it struck sharp on the inn door. We could hear the handle being turned, and the bolt rattling as the wretched being tried to enter; and then there was a long time of silence both within and without. At last the tapping recommenced and, to our indescribable joy and gratitude, died slowly away again down the road until it ceased to be heard.

We groped our way downstairs in the dark and ran out the door. As we surveyed the landscape that looked strangely eerie in the moonlight, the noise of tramping feet broke the silence of the night. Over the ridge, we could see a light tossing to and fro as it advanced, and in the light we saw three, four, maybe more, men advancing.

I knew that we must avoid the road so I moved my mother to a cove, hidden in the darkness that lay on the far side of the inn. I was sure we would not be seen there because I'd hidden there numerous times in my youth. Yet I found that I had outgrown the space, and my mother and I could not fit together there easily. But there we had to stay, within earshot of the inn.

My enemies began to arrive, seven or eight of them by the sound of their feet and shouting. The next moment I heard the tapping of the cane and the blind man's voice. He had returned with all these men!

"Down with the door!" he cried.

"Ay, ay, sir!" answered two or three; and a rush was made upon the Admiral Benbow. Four or five of them raced in.

"Bones is dead," I heard from inside.

"Search him, you shirking lubbers, and the rest of you get the chest," barked the blind man from outside.

The window of the captain's room was thrown open, and a man leaned out in the moonlight and addressed the blind beggar on the road below him.

"Someone's turned the chest out," he shouted.

"Is the map there?" roared the blind man.

"We don't see it here," returned the man.

"It's the people in the inn—it's that boy, he stole it. I wish I had put his eyes out!" He struck his stick against the side of the inn. "Rout the house out!"

Then there followed heavy feet pounding to and fro, furniture thrown over, doors kicked in, and finally the men, one after another, declared that we were nowhere to be found.

They began to quarrel among themselves, and suddenly from a distance I heard the sound of a pistol being shot off. The buccaneers turned at once and ran, separating in every direction. Only the blind man remained behind, tapping up and down the road in a frenzy, groping and calling for his comrades. Just then the noise of a horse was heard and a rider came into sight, sweeping at full gallop down the slope.

The blind man stumbled, and it was as though the rider only saw him at the last second, for he tried to turn his horse, but could not. Down went that cruel man with his stick, with a cry that rang high into the night. Four hooves trampled him quickly and he moved no more.

The rider slowed and stopped. It was Dr. Livesey. My mother and I climbed out of our hiding place.

"Who is that?" he shouted while dismounting.

I told him all that had happened.

"I felt remorse at having left you defenseless with that old drunk in the

At last the tapping recommenced and, to our indescribable joy and gratitude, died slowly away again down the road. . . .

house, so I returned with some help," said Dr. Livesey as a second rider drew alongside him. It was Squire Trelawney. He was a tall man, over six feet high, and broad in proportion, and he had a bluff, rough-and-ready face, all roughened and reddened and lined in his long sea travels. It was he who had fired the shot that had scattered the scavenging men.

"What were they after?" the squire asked.

I took from within my shirt the piece of paper and gave it to him.

Trelawney undid it slowly and looked at it. And though there was little light, I could tell from his expression that what he held was very important. It was a map of an island with latitude and longitude lines, and a hill marked THE SPY-GLASS.

He folded it quickly and said, "I don't think it is wise to remain in town. Doctor, this is Captain Flint's own map of a treasure too big to be imagined. We have all heard tall tales and sailors' stories of the fabled Treasure Island. And with this, we now know exactly where the island is, and where the treasure is buried! Tonight I will start for Bristol to find a ship."

"Excellent," replied Dr. Livesey after thinking for a moment. "I shall go with you, and Hawkins, you will come as a cabin boy. We'll take Redruth, Joyce, and Hunter. Squire, you must promise me that you will hold your tongue about all this. We are not the only men who know of this paper. Those fellows who attacked the inn tonight are determined to get this map. None of us must be alone until we get to sea. Jim and I shall stick together, you'll take Joyce and Hunter when you ride to Bristol, and from first to last, not one of us must breathe a word of what we've found."

"Livesey," returned the squire, "I'll be as silent as the grave."

CHAPTER FOUR

In the nights that followed, I found that my nightmares of a one-legged sailor were replaced by dreams of strange islands and adventures. I had studied the map by day, and in my dreams that lush, green island sprang to life. One night I would sail to the isle from one side, the next night the other, always exploring every acre of its surface. Every dream ended with me climbing the tall hill on the map called The Spy-glass.

At long last Redruth, a local gameskeeper, and I received a letter from the squire saying that he had purchased a ship called the *Hispaniola* and was fitting her with a crew. He also included in his postscript that he had signed on an experienced seaman as a cook, Long John Silver. We were to set sail soon!

In the days that passed between finding the map and setting off for Bristol, the squire saw to it that the Admiral Benbow was repaired as good as new so that my mother could again take on boarders. He had the sign repainted, added some new furniture, and even found her a boy as an apprentice so that she should not want for help while I was gone.

I said good-bye to Mother and the cove where I had lived since I was born, and to the dear old inn. I had an attack of fears, but regained my composure. Dr. Livesey joined us, and together with Redruth, we set off down the road, and soon the Benbow was out of sight.

We took a horse coach through the night to Bristol, where Trelawney had rented a room at an inn near the sea. In the morning, as we walked along the wharves, I saw many old sailors with rings in their ears, and whiskers curled into ringlets, and pigtails, and their swaggering, clumsy sea-walk. On one ship sailors were singing at their work; in another, there were men aloft, high over my head, hanging to threads that seemed no thicker than a spider's.

While I was still in this delightful dream of pigtailed seamen and of seeking buried treasure, we met Squire Trelawney.

"Good morning, cabin boy," he addressed me. "I need to run a note to John Silver. Take this here and, following the docks, keep a sharp lookout for a little tavern with a large brass telescope for a sign."

I found the tavern, entered, and was overwhelmed by dense tobacco smoke. The place was full of seafaring men. I asked at the counter for John Silver, and soon, out of a side room, came a one-legged man.

His left leg was cut off close to the hip, and under the left shoulder he carried a crutch, hopping about upon it like a bird. He was very tall and strong, with a face as big as a ham—plain and pale, but intelligent and smiling. Indeed, he seemed in the most cheerful spirits, whistling as he moved about the tables, with a merry word or a slap on the shoulder for the more favored of his guests.

From the first sight of him, I dreaded that he might be the very one-legged sailor I was to watch out for at the Admiral Benbow. But since I had seen Billy Bones, the blind man, and his ragged crew, I thought I knew what a buccaneer was like. This Long John Silver was different. He was clean, pleasant-tempered, and altogether unlike anything I imagined.

"Yes, my lad," said he, "you've been asking for Long John?" He took my hand in his large firm grasp. Immediately all of my past fears vanished under his smiling gaze.

"Squire Trelawney gave me a note to pass to you," I said as I handed him the paper.

"You're to be the cabin boy!" he exclaimed with a wide smile after he read the note. "Pleased I am to see you."

"It says here," he continued, "that I am to accompany you to our boat. Lead on, captain," he said, and laughed so heartily at his joke that I was obliged to join him. "You and me should get on well, Hawkins."

I said good-bye to Mother . . .

On our little walk along the quays, he made himself the most interesting companion, telling me about the different ships that we passed by; their rig and nationality; how one was discharging, another taking in cargo, and a third making ready for sea. I began to see that here was one of the best of possible shipmates.

When we got to the inn, we met the squire and Dr. Livesey.

"All hands aboard by four this afternoon," said the squire.

"Ay, ay, sir," cried Long John.

"Take your hat, Hawkins," the squire spoke as he got up, "and we'll see the ship."

CHAPTER FIVE

I won't relate the voyage to Treasure Island in much detail. The ship proved to be a good one, the crew of twenty-six were capable seamen, and the captain that the squire hired for the journey, Captain Smollett, thoroughly understood his business.

As for Long John Silver, the crew respected him and even obeyed him, even though he was only the ship's cook. To me he was continually kind, and always glad to see me in the galley. And I was always glad to see him and the parrot that he kept in a cage in the corner.

"I calls my parrot Cap'n Flint, after the famous buccaneer," Silver would say.

And the parrot would answer, "Pieces of eight! Pieces of eight!" I thought it curious that the bird would repeat the well-known pirate term for a golden coin, but once the voyage was underway, I was too busy in the ship's rigging, learning her ropes, to consider why the parrot would squawk so.

We took a course heading south-southwest toward Treasure Island, and had a steady breeze abeam and a quiet sea. Every one of us was in the bravest spirits because we felt as though we were near the end of our outward voyage.

Just after sundown one day, as I was on my way to my berth, it occurred to me that I would like an apple. I slipped into the empty galley and found I had to climb into the barrel to get the last of the apples. I sat for a moment in the barrel, examining an apple for signs of bruises, and recalled the tight cove my mother and I fit into outside of our inn the night the buccaneers ransacked it.

I was just about to stand and get out when I heard three men enter the room. From the scrape of a crutch upon the floor, I knew one of them to be Long John. The others, from the sound of their voices, were the deck mates Dick and Israel Hands.

What I heard from that moment on filled me with dread. I soon understood that the lives of all the honest men aboard depended upon me alone.

"We are gentlemen of fortune," Long John Silver began. "Israel Hands, here, and I like to eat and drink, fight, and end a voyage with more money than anyone else. And of anyone that gets in our way, well, we sends 'em to Davy Jones's locker at the bottom of the sea."

It took a moment before I understood the meaning of their terms. By "gentlemen of fortune," they plainly meant a common pirate; "Davy Jones's locker" meant death. And the little scene I was overhearing was probably the last act in the corruption of one of the honest hands left on board, Dick.

"Isn't that right?" Silver asked.

"I've had a'most enough o' Cap'n Smollett; he's hazed me long enough, by thunder! And I'm tired of smilin' and obeyin' him," Israel Hands said.

"Enough," Long John said, lowering his voice. "I'll finish with 'em at the island, as soon as the treasure's on board."

"But," asked Dick, "what do we do with the rest of 'em?"

"Dead men don't bite," said Israel.

"Right you are," said Long John. "I give my vote—death."

"So it's settled," Israel said. "Are you with us, Dick?"

"Ay," said the younger man.

"Good lad," encouraged Long John. "Now jump up and get me an apple."

You may imagine the terror I was in! I heard Dick begin to rise, and then someone seemingly stopped him, and the voice of Israel Hands exclaimed: "John, let's have a go of the rum." And with that, they departed the room.

After crouching for a long while in the barrel, I snuck my head up to see that the moon had risen. At almost the same time that I started to get out, the voice on the lookout shouted, "Land ho!"

I was always glad to see him and the parrot he kept in a cage by the corner.

CHAPTER SIX

*T*here was a great rush of feet across the deck as I slipped from my barrel and dived behind the foresail. I made toward the stern and came out upon the open deck in time to join Hunter and Dr. Livesey. A belt of fog had lifted almost simultaneously with the appearance of the moon. Away to the southwest we saw two low hills.

"Has any one of you ever seen that land ahead?" Captain Smollett shouted out to the crew.

"Yes, sir," replied Long John, "Skeleton Island they calls it. That big hill with the cloud on it—they usually calls that the Spy-glass."

So that was the Spy-glass, I thought. It looked larger and more mysterious than I had ever imagined it.

"Ah," Long John continued, "this here is a sweet spot, this island—a sweet spot for a lad to get ashore on." And clapping me in the friendliest way upon the shoulder, he hobbled off forward and went below. I was surprised at the coolness with which John related his knowledge of the island, and could scarce conceal a shudder when he had laid his hand upon me.

"Doctor," I said, anxious to tell my story, "let me speak. Get the captain and squire down to the cabin, and then make some pretense to send for me. I have terrible news."

The doctor's countenance changed a little.

"Thank you, Jim," he said, quite loudly, "that was all I wanted to know," as if he had asked me a question. And with that he turned on his heel and approached Captain Smollett and Squire Trelawney. Then the three gentlemen went below, and not long afterward, word was sent that I was wanted in the cabin.

Loaded pistols were served out to all the sure men. . . .

I found them all seated round the table, and behind them, out the window, you could see the moon shining on the ship's wake.

"Now, Hawkins," said the squire, "you have something to say. Speak up."

I told them the whole details of Silver's conversation. When I was through, the captain spoke up. "I see three or four points in regards to the situation we are now in. First, we must go on, because if I gave the word to turn around, they would rise at once. Second, we have time until the treasure is found. Third, there are faithful hands aboard. I'm sure Hunter, Joyce, and Redruth will stand with us."

"Jim, here," the doctor piped in, "can help us more than anyone. The men are not shy with him, and Jim is a noticing lad."

I took enormous pride that these fine men would place their trust in me. Pride, but also fear. For of the twenty-six men on board, our force equaled only seven. Seven against nineteen hardened and murderous men.

The appearance of the island when I came on deck the next morning was altogether changed. With its grey, melancholy woods, wild stone spires, and sweltering heat, I began to hate the very thought of Treasure Island. The captain sailed the *Hispaniola* to just where the anchor was in the chart, about a third of a mile from each shore, the mainland on one side, and Skeleton Island on the other. Because of the thick trees, we could see nothing of the house and stockade that were in the southeast corner of the island on the map.

The mood of the men on the ship had turned dark. The slightest order was received with a black look, and grudgingly and carelessly obeyed.

The captain took note of this and held a council of the honest men in his cabin. Loaded pistols were served out to all the sure men, and then Captain Smollett went on deck and addressed the crew.

"My lads," he said, "we've had a hot day and are all tired and out of sorts. Go ashore and I'll fire a gun a half an hour before sundown for you to return."

The men all came out of their sulks in a moment and gave a cheer. The captain whipped out of sight, leaving Long John Silver to arrange the party. Had he been on deck, he would have had to pretend to not understand the situation. It was as plain as day. To all the mutineers, Long John was the captain.

At last the disembarking party was made up. Six fellows were to stay on board, and the remaining thirteen, including Long John, began to fill the two boats.

Then it came into my head that if six men were to be left on board by Long John, the men loyal to the captain could not take back the ship, their numbers being the same as ours, six versus six. I was sure no mutiny would occur just yet, though. The men loyal to Long John would wait till he returned before they attempted to take the ship.

Still, with the heat and lack of wind, I could not stand to be on the boat any longer. It sprung into my mind to go ashore. In a jiffy I slipped over the side and curled up in the foresheets of the nearest boat, and almost at the same moment she shoved off.

No one took notice of me, and the boat I was in, being lighter and better manned, shot far ahead of the other. When the bow had struck among the shoreside trees, I caught a branch and swung myself out, and plunged into the nearest thicket.

"Jim, Jim!" I heard Silver shouting. But I paid no heed, and I ran until I could run no longer.

I was so pleased at having given the slip to Long John, that I began to enjoy myself and look around. I now felt for the first time the joy of exploration. Here and there were flowering plants, unknown to me, as well as large oaks, a steaming marsh, and a vast thicket of twisted and rambling foliage. As I surveyed Spy-glass Hill in the distance, a bustle erupted in the marsh, sending a great cloud of screaming birds overhead.

I instantly crouched, then crawled under cover of an oak and squatted there, silent as a mouse. Then I heard Silver's voice among his men. It was in the distance, but I could hear a commotion and shouting. Crawling on all fours, I made steadily but slowly toward them. Far away out in the marsh there arose, all of a sudden, a sound like the cry of anger, then another, and then one horrid, long-drawn scream.

Then, from the other side of the marsh, I saw Silver with a small group of men. Tom, one of the men with Silver, leaped at the sound, but Silver did not wink an eye.

"Long John!" said Tom. "What in heaven's name was that?"

"That?" returned Silver, smiling away. "Oh, I reckon that'll be one of Captain Smollett's men—Alan."

"Alan!" cried Tom. "He was as true a seaman as there ever was. John Silver, you're no mate of mine. You've killed Alan, have you? Kill me, too, if you can."

And with that, he turned his back directly on the cook. But he was not destined to go far. With a cry, John took up his crutch and struck poor Tom with stunning violence. Tom gave a sort of gasp, and fell. Silver, agile as a cat, was on top of him the next moment, and had twice buried his knife into his defenseless body.

I fell backward in amazement, and the whole world seemed to swim away from before me.

When I came again to myself, I ran clear of the thicket, scarce minding the direction of my flight, so long as it led me from the murderers. As I ran, I thought it was all over. Good-bye to the *Hispaniola;* good-bye to the squire, the doctor, and the captain! There was nothing left for me but death by starvation, or death by the hands of the mutineers. And so I ran until a fresh alarm brought me to a standstill with a thumping heart.

I saw a figure, dark and shaggy like a monkey, leap behind the trunk of a pine tree.

CHAPTER SEVEN

I saw a figure, dark and shaggy like a monkey, leap behind the trunk of a pine tree. The terror of this new apparition stopped me short. Instantly the figure reappeared. From trunk to trunk the creature flitted like a deer, running manlike on two legs, but unlike any man that I had ever seen, stooping almost double as it ran.

Then, from behind a tree trunk, it leaped directly at me! I froze in my tracks as we stood face-to-face.

"Who are you?" I asked, trembling.

"I'm poor Ben Gunn, I am, and I haven't spoke with a man these three years."

I could now see that he was a white man like myself. His skin was burnt by the sun, even his lips were black, and his fair eyes looked quite startling in so dark a face. He was clothed in tatters of old ships' canvas and sea cloth.

"Three years!" I cried. "Were you shipwrecked?"

"Nay, mate," said he—"marooned."

I had heard the word, and I knew it stood for a horrible kind of punishment in which the offender is put ashore on some desolate and distant island by buccaneers.

"What do you call yourself, mate?" he asked.

"Jim," I told him.

"Now, Jim," he began. "That ship anchored off the shore, is it a pirate ship?"

"It may be soon if a cook among us has his way," I replied truthfully.

"A cook? Not a man—with one—leg?" he gasped.

"Silver?" I asked, curious that he might know our chief mutineer.

"Ah, Silver!" he said. "That was his name. Years ago I sailed with Captain Flint on the *Walrus*. With us were the coldhearted Long John Silver as quartermaster, and that drunk Billy Bones as the mate. Well, mind you, Jim, Captain Flint went ashore this island with six strong seamen to bury his stolen treasure. And only Flint returned to the ship. The rest were murdered. Later on that voyage I heard Silver say that he would do whatever necessary to return to this island and someday get the treasure."

"And so he has," I said.

"Ay, he has, but there's more," said Ben. "Three years back while I sailed with another crew, I sighted this island by chance. I told the men that there was a treasure here. And for twelve days we searched for it, for we had no map, you see. One fine morning they left me here with only a musket for a friend. They had grown tired of looking and so deserted me without finding the treasure."

At this point the ragged man before me looked longingly out to the sea and said softly, "How I would love to climb aboard your ship and sail faraway from here."

"I as well," I said, "but there is no way to get back on board."

"Ah," Gunn smiled, "there's my boat, that I made with my two hands. I keep her under the white rock. We might try that after dark."

I was about to tell him that only a handful of honest men kept the ship from full mutiny, when the cannon fired from the ship. Immediately we heard pistol and musket fire from across the island.

"They have begun to fight!" I cried, and together we ran toward the sound of the gunfire. It was nearly a half an hour through thick forest growth before Ben and I came to an opening at the bottom of a knoll. At the top was a log house, still in admirable shape. All around this, down the hill a way, was cleared a wide space, and a stockade had been erected with a wall of tree trunks six feet high.

A number of gun barrels stuck out from the log house and began to fire. They were answered by a volley of small arms from the forest across the clearing from us. Yet I could not see who was in the stockade and who was firing from the woods. After another round was fired, the group in the wood seemed to retreat, for I did not hear any more gunshot or see any more smoke.

And then I saw above the log house a flag being raised; it was the Union Jack, and I realized that my friends had made it to safety.

As soon as Ben Gunn saw the colors flying above the stockade house he said, "There are your friends, sure enough. Silver would fly the pirate flag, the Jolly Roger. Tell me, Jim, do you think your friends would help an old one like myself to be free from here?"

I told him that I was sure they would. When he heard this, he smiled.

"I must go now. I have a score to settle with old Silver," he said. "But when you need me, you can find me where we first met."

I said good-bye to Ben and moved toward the stockade. From my hiding place I could see the shore. On the beach were a number of the mutineers demolishing one of the *Hispaniola*'s boats. I assumed it was the one that my friends had used to row ashore. I rose to my feet, confident that they could not see me, and saw some distance further down the reef an isolated rock that was peculiarly white in color. It occurred to me that this might be the white rock where Ben Gunn had hid his boat.

I skirted the woods, approached the stockade, bounded over the wall, and was soon warmly received by the faithful party.

"Jim," Dr. Livesey said excitedly, "we heard a scream onshore and thought it was you."

"No," I said, "that was Alan."

"When we heard it, we knew we had to come onshore. Had there been a wind, we would have fought the men on board, pulled up an anchor, and sailed far from here. But as there isn't, we knew by nightfall that Silver and his

And then I saw above the log house a flag being raised. . . .

men would come back aboard and take the ship for themselves. Our only choice was to row to the island and make it to this stockade that we saw on the map. We made it here, but not without a fight. Gray, Hunter, Trelawney, Joyce, the captain, and I survived. Tom Redruth is lying in the log house, shot dead by one of Silver's men."

When I entered, I saw his body on the floor, covered by another of the ship's British flags.

Captain Smollett divided us into watches: the doctor, Gray, and I, for one; the squire, Hunter, and Joyce for the other. Tired though we all were, two were sent out for firewood; two more were sent to dig a grave for Redruth. I was put sentry at the door.

I told the doctor about Ben Gunn, and he was glad to hear that we might have another friend on the island.

The day passed slowly, for it was very hot and I was very tired. When at last I was able to sleep, I slept like a log.

In the morning I was awakened by a flurry of voices beyond the wall.

The captain looked on for a while in silence. Then he spoke: "My lads, we are outnumbered, and I fear this stockade will be boarded. Gather together our munitions."

We brought our muskets, ammunition, and cutlasses into the log house and laid them on the table. And just at that moment the first musket ball flew over our heads. Joyce quickly whipped his musket from the table and fired. I did not know if he struck anything, for we were rapidly grasping our weapons as several more bullets came from the woods and struck the log house. By the time I reached the door, the mutineers were already swarming like monkeys over the stockade fence. Squire and Gray fired, grabbed another musket, then fired again. Three men fell. Four more headed directly for the building, shouting as they ran.

. . . the mutineers were already swarming like monkeys over the stockade fence.

A pirate grasped Hunter's musket by the muzzle and, with one stunning blow, laid the poor fellow senseless on the floor. Another, running unharmed all round the outside of the house, appeared suddenly in the doorway and attacked the doctor with his cutlass.

"Out, lads, out, and fight 'em in the open! Cutlasses!" cried the captain.

I snatched a cutlass from the pile and dashed out of the door into the clear sunlight. In front of me, the doctor was pursuing his assailant and sent him sprawling on his back, with a great slash across his face. I was looking for Silver to deliver his death blow, but then thought that he would be too big a coward to climb the wall again and fight with his men.

"Round the house, lads! Round the house!" cried the captain, and even in the hurly-burly of the fight I perceived a change in his voice.

Already the tide of the battle was turning in our favor. A number of Silver's men lay inside the stockade. The last mutineer made his escape and disappeared into the woods. In several seconds nothing remained of the attacking party but the five who had fallen.

We returned to the house and saw at a glance the price we had paid for victory. Hunter lay stunned, while Joyce was shot in the head, never to move again. The squire was supporting the captain, one as pale as the other.

"The captain's wounded," said Mr. Trelawney.

And so, out of the eight men who had fallen, only three still breathed: one of the pirates, Hunter, and Captain Smollett. Unfortunately, as the hours passed, Hunter fared worse and worse, and he never regained consciousness. As for the captain, his wounds were grievous indeed, but not dangerous. A shot had broken his shoulder blade and touched the lung. He was sure to recover, but for weeks to come, he must not walk nor move his arm.

"They will think twice before attacking us again," the captain said with a hint of pride in his voice.

After lunch the squire and the doctor sat and talked. Afterward Doctor Livesey took up his hat and pistols, grabbed a cutlass, put the map in his pocket, and with a musket over his shoulder crossed over the wooden fence and set off briskly through the trees.

"I take it," I said to Gray, knowing that Livesey would never betray us, "that the doctor is going now to see Ben Gunn."

As the midday sun grew in intensity, I began to envy the doctor, walking in the cool shadow of the woods, with the birds about him, while I sat grilling with so much blood about me. I made up my mind to get out.

I laid hold of a couple of pistols, a powder-horn and bullets, and some biscuits, and I was off. While the squire and Gray were busy helping the captain with his bandages, I made a bolt for it over the stockade and into the thickest of the trees. I headed straight for the east coast of the island.

Soon cool drafts of air began to reach me, and there, in the open borders of the grove, lay the sea, blue and sunny to the horizon. From where I hid, I could see the *Hispaniola* offshore with Silver and a few men boarding a smaller boat alongside. And as the sun fell behind Spy-glass Hill they set off for shore. I saw I must lose no time if I were to find Gunn's boat that evening.

The white rock, visible enough above the brush, was still about an eighth of a mile farther down the shore. It took me a while to get to it, often crawling on all fours among the scrub. Night had almost come when I laid my hands on its rough sides. Right below it there was a small hollow, and in the center of the dell was a little tent of goatskins. I dropped into the hollow, lifted the side of the tent, and there was Ben Gunn's small boat.

My plan was to slip out under cover of the night, cut the *Hispaniola* adrift, and let her go ashore wherever she pleased. I felt that this was the best way to deny the mutineers onshore a chance to escape out to sea. If they took the ship back to England, there was no doubt in my mind that they would make up a story as to how we all died. Then no rescue boat would ever be sent to us.

As the last rays of daylight dwindled and disappeared, absolute blackness settled down on Treasure Island. I began to paddle away from the island.

First the *Hispaniola* loomed before me like a blot, blacker than the darkness, then her spars and hull began to take shape. Soon I was alongside of her. I paddled to her back side and heard the sound of angry voices from above. It was Israel Hands and another sailor in the captain's cabin.

Curses flew like hailstones, and every now and then there came forth such verbal explosions that I thought it was sure to end in blows. I found the anchor rope where it shot into the water and drew out my cutlass. I cut clear through; the ship lurched forward and, free of its holdings, swung toward me. My boat was almost instantly swept against the bow of the *Hispaniola*.

I paddled hard, for I expected at any moment to be drawn under the much larger ship. My vessel began to take on water. I knew that if I stayed here, or leaped into the water, I would be drawn into the tide of the moving ship and killed. I scrambled for the loose anchor line and began to climb up it, pulling myself up the cord, hand over hand, toward the captain's cabin.

The now-moving ship made plenty of noise slapping against the waves, but until I got my eye above the windowsill, I could not comprehend why the watchmen had taken no alarm. One glance was sufficient. It showed me Israel Hands and his companion locked together in a deadly wrestle.

Suddenly the schooner gave a violent yaw, turning perhaps twenty degrees. I could hear feet pounding on the companion ladder, and I knew that the two drunkards had at last been interrupted in their quarrel and awakened to a sense of their disaster. I started to lower myself back down toward Gunn's tiny skiff when I heard the crack of wood against wood. My boat had been drawn under the schooner! I was left without retreat on the *Hispaniola*.

It showed me Israel Hands and his companion locked together in a deadly wrestle.

It was broad day when I awoke, and I could see the strains of sunlight stream through the canvas that I had hid under the night before. Though I heard much yelling and scurrying throughout the night, I dared not show myself. I don't know how much I slept between my prayers that the ship would not wander off to sea.

It was quiet on deck when I peeked out from my hiding place. I saw that we were sailing adrift at the southwest end of Treasure Island. For a while the ship kept bucking and sidling like a vicious horse. I looked up and saw that the *Hispaniola*'s half-drawn mainsail and two jibs were merely shivering in the breeze.

Then, on the deck, not far from where I was, I saw one of the men lying face down in a pool of blood, and the other, Israel Hands, propped against the bulwarks, his face as white as sun-bleached driftwood. He turned partly around and, with a low moan, writhed himself into a sitting position. It was apparent that he been struck numerous times by the blood that had soaked into his clothes.

I walked aft until I reached the mainmast and stood before him.

"Come aboard, Mr. Hands," I said, ironically.

He rolled his eyes round heavily.

"And where might you have come from?" he asked through parched lips.

"I've come aboard to take possession of this ship, Mr. Hands, and you'll please regard me as your captain until further notice."

He looked at me sourly. "I reckon, Cap'n Hawkins, you'll want to get ashore, now."

"Why, yes," I said. "But I'm not going back to Captain Flint's anchorage. I mean for you to sail us into the North Inlet."

"To be sure," he cried. "I haven't no choice! I'll help you sail her."

In ten minutes I had the *Hispaniola* sailing easily before the wind along the coast of Treasure Island. Since the wind was not too strong, and did not change direction, I had little problem handling the schooner nearly single-handedly. Soon we turned the corner of the island on the north and sailed into the North Inlet. I was happy with my new command and pleased with the bright, sunshiny weather.

Israel Hands told me how to lay the ship to, and after a good many trials I succeeded. He scarcely moved from where he sat. And though he appeared helpless, I knew his thoughts and his heart were full of deceit. He referred to me nicely as "cap'n" and "sir," but I knew he was storing his strength. I was sure he would not make a move until we were anchored and safe within the inlet, for he still needed me to sail the ship to safety. I resolved to carry my two pistols in the inner pockets of my coat, out of sight in case his strength returned.

"Now," said Hands when we drew near the shore, "let's beach the ship."

"And once beached," I inquired, "how shall we get her off again?"

"You take a line ashore there on the other side at low water, take a turn about one o' them big pines, bring it back, take a turn round the capstan, and lie-to for the tide. Come high water, all hands take a pull upon the line, and off she comes as smooth as butter."

So he issued commands which I obeyed. At last the ship stopped upon a bank of sand. I was so caught up in my pride of successfully landing the *Hispaniola* that I was surprised when Hands leaped forward. He grabbed the knife from under the body of the man he murdered, and lunged. He threw himself at me, and I leaped sideways toward the bow. Wounded as he was, it was amazing how fast he could move.

I was about to draw my pistols out when suddenly a wave took the *Hispaniola* and canted her over to the port side, till the deck stood at an angle of forty-five degrees. We were both capsized in a second, rolling down the deck.

Quick as a shot, I regained my feet and sprang into the mizzen shrouds. Hand over hand I climbed and did not draw a breath till I was seated on the crosstrees. When I looked down, I saw Israel Hands with a knife in his mouth following me up. He groaned as he hauled his wounded leg behind him.

After priming my pistols, one in each hand, I addressed him: "One more step, Mr. Hands, and I'll blow your brains out!"

In a flash his right hand went over his shoulder, and something like an arrow sang through the air. I felt a blow and then a sharp pang. I was pinned by the shoulder to the mast with a knife! In the horrid pain and surprise of the moment, both my pistols went off. My pursuer, and would-be murderer, loosened his grasp upon the shrouds and plunged headfirst into the water, dead.

I began to feel sick, faint, and terrified. Hot blood was running over my back and chest; the knife burned like a hot iron. I was terrified of falling from the crosstrees, and my first thought was to pull out the blade. On inspection I found that the knife, in fact, had come the nearest in the world to missing me altogether; it held me by a mere pinch of skin. I plucked it out with a sudden jerk and a yell.

I climbed down the mast and went below to do what I could for my wound. To my relief I saw that it was neither deep nor dangerous. I washed away the blood and headed back above. I was now alone on the ship. The tide had just turned and the ship began to straighten itself onto an even keel. And as the tide went out the schooner settled herself nicely on her beam-ends.

I was confident that the boat would be safe here in the inlet because the pirates would have no idea where it was now hidden, far from its original anchorage.

I dropped overboard. The water scarcely reached my waist, and I waded ashore in great spirits. When I reached the woods, I set my face toward the blockhouse and my companions and began walking. Careful to remain hidden

from any pirates who might be patrolling, it took me most of the afternoon to return to where I had last left my friends.

The moon was beginning to rise in the evening sky when I reached the stockade and silently leaped over the fence. But right in front of me, a glow of a different color appeared among the trees. It was the embers of a bonfire smoldering. It was Captain Smollett's orders not to build great fires, and so I thought it strange that one should be burning now. I began to fear that something had gone wrong while I was absent.

I got on my hands and knees and crawled without a sound toward the corner of the house. As I drew nearer, my heart was suddenly and greatly lightened. It was like music to my ears to hear my friends snoring together so loud and peaceful in their sleep.

All's well, I thought.

But there was no doubt of one thing, they kept a terribly bad watch. If it had been Silver and his lads that were now creeping in on them, not a soul would have seen daybreak. I blamed myself sharply for leaving them in that danger with so few to mount guard.

By this time I had got to the door and stood up. All was dark. I walked in. I thought it might be funny to lie down in my own place and see the faces of my friends when they awoke the next morning to find me asleep next to them.

And then, all of a sudden, a shrill noise broke forth out of the darkness: "Pieces of eight! Pieces of eight!"

It was Silver's green parrot, Cap'n Flint, that was keeping better watch than any human being.

"Who goes?" Silver cried out.

I turned to run, struck violently against one person, recoiled, and ran full into the arms of a second, who, for his part, closed upon me and held me tight.

Chapter Eight

*T*he red glare of the torch lighting up the interior of the blockhouse showed me the worst of my fears realized. The pirates were in possession of the house and all the food supplies. I could only judge that all my friends had been killed.

I stood there, looking Silver in the face, pluckily enough I hoped to all outward appearance, but with black despair in my heart.

Silver took a whiff or two of his pipe before he spoke.

"Now, you see, Jim, I've always liked you. I always wanted you to join and take your share, and now you've got to. Your friends are still alive, but they've been banished, as it were. When they saw that the *Hispaniola* was gone, they gave up hope, and so I traded them all the food here for their freedom."

I was glad to hear that the others were still alive, but I tried to be as calm in my expressions as was Silver.

"And now you are to choose," he finished. "Are you loyal to them, or do you throw your lot in with us?"

"Well," I said. "There's a thing or two I have to tell you. You are in a bad way and I know it. Ship lost, treasure lost, men lost . . . and if you want to know who did it, it was I!"

I saw the faces of the men come alive in amazement as my speech became more and more impassioned.

"I was in the apple barrel and I heard you. As for the schooner, it was I who cut her cable, and it was I who killed the men you had aboard her. The laugh's on my side; I've had the top of this business from the first, and I no more fear you than I fear a fly."

Although the men started to grumble, Silver sat there, still smoking, and I could not tell whether or not he had been impressed with my courage. Morgan, drawing his knife, sprang at me. Silver stopped him with a shout.

"Avast, there!" the cook called out. "Maybe you thought you was cap'n here."

Morgan paused, and the murmuring among the men grew louder.

"Morgan's right," said one.

"Did any of you gentlemen want to have it out with me?" roared Silver.

Not a man stirred; not a man answered.

"You won't touch Jim because I like the boy. I've never seen a better boy than that. He's more a man than any pair of rats of you in this here house."

There was a long pause after this. My heart was going like a sledgehammer at this point, for I knew my life held in the balance.

The men drew gradually together toward the far end of the blockhouse, until at last one came forward and spoke to Silver.

"I ask your pardon, sir, acknowledging you to be cap'n at this house, but I claim my right which is to step outside for a council." And then he stepped toward the door and disappeared out of the house. One after another, the rest followed his example. All marched out and left Silver and me alone with the torch.

The sea-cook instantly removed his pipe.

"Now, look you here, Jim Hawkins, they're going to throw me off. I'll save your life if I can. But, see here, Jim, you must save Long John from swinging."

"If we get out of here, I'll do what I can," I said truthfully.

I peered out the window and saw about halfway down the slope to the stockade fence the pirates collected in a group. One was on his knees with the blade of an open knife in his hand. When one looked my way, I ducked down.

In a few moments they reentered the house. A buccaneer stepped forward and gave a piece of paper to Long John. The sea-cook and I looked at what had been given him. On one side was written the word "deposed." Beneath that

One was on his knees with the blade of an open knife in his hand.

was the mark of a black spot made with wood ash. It was the very same mark that Billy Bones had been given at the Admiral Benbow Inn.

"The black spot!" Silver observed.

George, the leader of the council, stepped forward to list their grievances.

"First, you've made a hash of this voyage. Second, you let the enemy out o' this here trap for nothing. Third, you wouldn't let us finish them off. And then, fourth, there's this here boy."

"Is that all?" asked Silver quietly, taking from his vest a piece of paper. It was none other than the treasure map on yellow paper, with the three crosses on it that I had found in Billy Bones's sea chest. The doctor must have given it to him in exchange for safe passage from the stockade.

The appearance of the chart clearly was an incredible sight to the surviving mutineers. They leaped upon it like cats upon a mouse.

"Mighty nice," said George. "But how are we to get away with it, and us with no ship?"

"Here's the pretty part," said Silver. "Before we left port, the doctor made sure that if our boat did not return after a certain date, another one would sail for this island to find the *Hispaniola*. If I hadn't traded the doctor's life for this map and food, we'd soon be dead."

I looked about at the men and could tell by their expressions that they were again loyal to Silver.

"Now all we need to do is find the treasure and wait for our ship to arrive. And to be sure there's no trouble, we keeps Jim here as a hostage."

CHAPTER NINE

In the morning we set out for treasure. We made a curious-looking troop, all in soiled sailor clothes, and all but me armed to the teeth. Silver had two guns slung about him, one in front and one behind. He also carried a great cutlass at his wrist, and a pistol in each pocket of his square-tailed coat.

I had a line around my waist and followed obediently after the sea-cook, who held the loose end of the rope. For all to see, I was led like a dancing bear.

The other men carried picks and shovels, as well as pork, bread, and brandy for a midday meal. We made our way to the beach where the small boats the pirates originally had sailed in on lay. After we got in and had been rowing for a while, Silver took out the map and studied it some more.

At length, we landed at the mouth of a river that ran near Spy-glass Hill. We disembarked and began to ascend the slope toward the plateau.

We walked until the men grew tired in the noonday heat. We sat in some shade as Silver took certain bearings with his compass.

All of a sudden, out of the middle of the trees in front of us, a thin, high, trembling voice rang out:

> "Fifteen men on the dead man's chest—
> Yo-ho-ho, and a bottle of rum!"

The color went from the faces of the six pirates. They would have run separately had they dared, but fear kept them together.

"It's a spirit," said George.

Then a light of recognition came to Silver's face.

"By the powers, it's Ben Gunn!" he roared. "I sailed with him on the *Walrus!*"

"It don't make much difference," Dick said. "Ben Gunn's not alive."

"But nobody here minds Ben Gunn," cried Long John. "Dead or alive."

It was extraordinary how their spirits had returned when they witnessed Silver's lack of fear. Instantly the natural color had returned to their faces.

Silver got us walking again as he spoke of the treasure. The thought of the money swallowed up their previous terrors. Their eyes burned in their heads, their feet grew speedier and lighter, and their whole soul was bound up in that fortune.

Then we came to a clearing.

"Huzza, mates, all together!" shouted Morgan, and then broke into a run. The other men followed after him. Then suddenly, not ten yards farther, they stopped. A low cry arose.

Silver and I brought up the rear. Before us lay a great excavation. In this gaping hole in the ground was the shaft of a pick broken in two and some old boards. On one of these boards I saw, branded with a hot iron, "Walrus"—the name of Flint's ship.

It was clear as daylight to all present: the cache had been found, and all seven hundred thousand pounds were gone!

Each of these six men was as though he had been struck. But with Silver, the blow passed almost instantly. He kept his head, found his even temper, and changed his plan before the others had had time to realize the disappointment.

"Jim," he whispered as he passed me a double-barreled pistol, "take that, and stand by for trouble."

The buccaneers, with curses and cries, began to leap, one after another, into the pit, and to dig with their fingers. When they found nothing, they climbed out.

There we stood, two on one side, five on the other, the pit between us, and nobody with the guts to offer the first blow.

Then Morgan got a look in his eyes that left no debate to his intentions. He raised his cutlass and began to charge us when—*Crack! Crack! Crack!* Three

Silver and I brought up the rear.

musket shots flashed out of the thicket. Morgan dropped his blade and tumbled headfirst into the excavation. Another pirate was hit and fell to the earth, twitching as life passed from him.

Before you could wink, Long John also fired two barrels at the struggling Morgan. Even in the excitement, I was sickened by the sight of Silver firing into the body of an unarmed, defenseless man.

At that moment Doctor Livesey and Gray joined us, with smoking barrels, from among the nutmeg trees.

The other three pirates turned and ran with all their might.

"Stop them," I shouted. "The boats!"

"No need to worry, lad," said the doctor. "They're running in the wrong direction."

Silver piped up, "Thank ye kindly, doctor. You came in about the nick of time, I guess, for me and Hawkins."

The doctor made no reply and merely stared at the cook who was, just a few moments ago, the leader of the mutineers. Ben parted the foliage and stepped out for Silver to see.

"And so it is you, Ben Gunn!" he added. "Well, you're a fine fellow to see."

"How do you do, Mr. Silver?" replied the maroon.

"Ben, Ben," murmured Silver, "to think that you're the one who did me in. You were shown the map by one of these men, weren't you? You found the treasure, and it made the map here useless." He smiled, resigned to the fact that Gunn turned out to be a better thief than he. "So *that's* why the doctor gave it to me in exchange for his life and the life of his men. You must have been in cahoots together on this island."

I don't know what Ben Gunn thought at that moment, but he had a smile so wide that I couldn't help thinking that he was proud that it was he who out-maneuvered one of the most treacherous pirates ever, Long John Silver.

We left the excavation and the two dead pirates, made our way to the shore, and got into one of the boats. The doctor demolished the other one with a pickax. Then we set out for the North Inlet by sea.

We found the *Hispaniola* about three miles into the North Inlet. The tide had lifted her off the sand, and without a strong wind to blow her away, she merely bobbed in the tranquil blue waters of the inlet.

We pulled round and found a gentle slope that ran up from the beach to the entrance of the cave where Gunn had hid the treasure.

It was a large, airy place with a little spring and a pool of clear water, overhung with ferns. The floor was sand. Before a big fire lay Captain Smollett, and in a far corner, I beheld great heaps of coins of nearly every variety of money in the world.

This was Flint's treasure! And it had already cost the lives of seventeen men from the *Hispaniola*. I did not dare venture to guess how many other men lost their lives over this money.

CHAPTER TEN

*T*he morning we set sail for home was bright and the island never looked nicer, now that we were leaving it. The treasure took us three days to load. We also made a point to stock plenty of goat's flesh and water for the trip back.

As we sailed out of the inlet, we saw the three mutineers kneeling on a knoll, with their arms raised as though begging us to take them with us. We had earlier decided not to take them for fear of another mutiny. Silver came along with us though, much to the doctor's dismay. But he had saved my life in the stockade, and I pledged him my word that I would keep him from the noose.

However, he did not stay with us long. One night when we stopped in a South American port, the one-legged (and two-faced) cook and mutineer must have found his way to shore. He took with him a sack of gold. We were glad to be rid of him so cheaply. Curiously, he did not take his parrot, Cap'n Flint, with him. Throughout the voyage home to Bristol, the bird squawked.

And so it is whenever I think of my adventures and the fortune I helped find, I always hear from somewhere in my memory: "Pieces of eight! Pieces of eight!"

This was Flint's treasure!